FOGBOUND

FOGBOUND

written and illustrated by
STEVEN SHEPARD

LANDMARK EDITIONS, INC.
P.O. Box 4469 • 1402 Kansas Avenue • Kansas City, Missouri 64127

I am deeply grateful to everyone
who made this book possible:

My grandparents Robert and Eugenia Shepard,
who own the white farmhouse by Moffat Cove
and make my summers there so pleasant;

My caring and supportive parents
Andrew and Judith Shepard,
both of whom I love very much;

And those who posed for the illustrations—
Rachel Knobloch, Juliet Leonard,
Barclay Shepard and Ben Shepard.

COPYRIGHT © 1993 STEVEN SHEPARD

International Standard Book Number: 0-933849-43-5 (LIB.BDG.)

Library of Congress Cataloging-in-Publication Data
Shepard, Steven, 1978-
    Fogbound / written and illustrated by Steven Shepard.
    p.   cm.
    Summary: When twelve-year-old Jason rows his boat to the Maine island
where he has accidentally left his father's knife, he must face threatening fog,
treacherous currents, and a sinister lobsterman.
    ISBN 0-933849-43-5 (lib.bdg. : acid-free paper)
  1. Children's writings, American.
  [1. Adventure and Adventurers—Fiction.
  2. Boats and boating—Fiction.   3. Islands—Fiction.
  4. Maine—Fiction.   5. Children's writings.]
  I. Title.   II. Title: Fog bound
  PZ7.S54327Fo   1993
  [Fic]—dc20   93-13422
                                      CIP
                                      AC

Editorial Coordinator: Nancy R. Thatch
Creative Coordinator: David Melton

Printed in the United States of America

Landmark Editions, Inc.
P.O. Box 4469
1402 Kansas Avenue
Kansas City, Missouri 64127
(816) 241-4919

FOGBOUND

In his exciting adventure story, Steven Shepard deftly takes readers into the mind of a fourteen-year-old boy named Jason. There, we become involved in the boy's thoughts, his schemes, his deceptions, his desperation, and his inevitable confrontation with his own conscience.

Steven is a very skillful writer who doesn't move blithely from one sentence to another. Instead, he builds his story so each thought flows smoothly into another and each piece of action builds upon the next one. In short, his approach is precise, and his story structure is impeccable.

Working with Steven was a very interesting experience to say the least. He definitely has a mind of his own, and he certainly is not shy about expressing his opinions and ideas, which are many. But he also has the good sense to consider constructive suggestions and the extraordinary desire to improve his work. He was willing to spend whatever hours were required to embellish the text of FOGBOUND. And the improvements he made in his skills as an illustrator astonished his parents and certainly pleased me.

A good book doesn't just happen. It requires determination, energy, and skill on the part of its author and illustrator. Now you have the opportunity to read and experience the results of Steven's hours of work and enjoy his creative genius.

— David Melton

Creative Coordinator
Landmark Editions, Inc.

WINNER

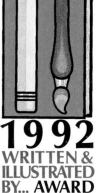

1992
WRITTEN &
ILLUSTRATED
BY... AWARD

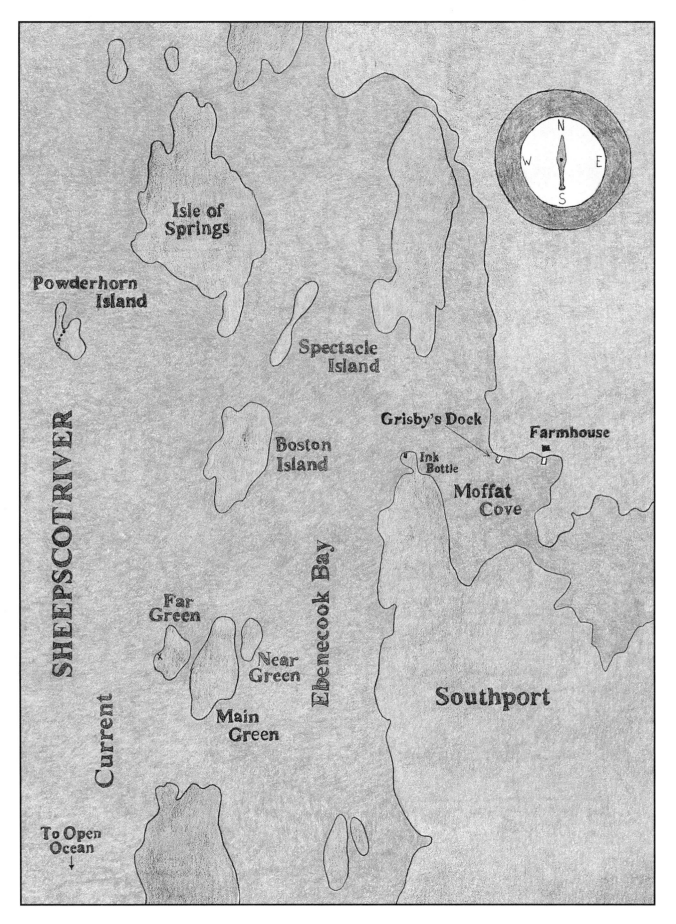

Isle of
Springs

Powderhorn
Island

Spectacle
Island

SHEEPSCOT RIVER

Grisby's Dock

Farmhouse

Ink
Bottle

Moffat
Cove

Boston
Island

Ebenecook Bay

Current

Far
Green

Near
Green

Southport

Main
Green

To Open
Ocean

The old white farmhouse on the coast of Maine has been in our family for five generations. For as long as I can remember, we have journeyed there to spend our summers in the crisp air and calm seas of Moffat Cove, near Boothbay Harbor.

Each day we would wake to the cries of gulls and the sounds of the gentle surf. We'd while away the hours among the fields and rocks along the coast. Ours was the perfect summer home, peaceful and idyllic. Nothing threatening, or even out of the ordinary, ever happened to us there — that is, not until one Friday when I was twelve years old.

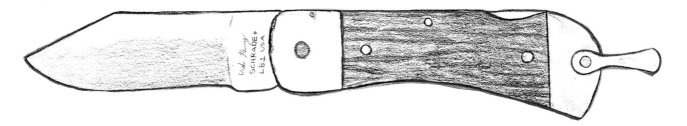

When I awoke that Friday, my first thought was of the knife — a blade of steel, smooth and polished, oiled just enough to slide open and lock. It was perfect for whittling wood and gutting fish. It was my father's knife. I shouldn't have taken it the day before. But I did.

Yesterday morning the knife had been too tempting to me as it lay there on Father's bureau. I wanted to show it to my friends — Joe and Ben McClosky. So I took it, just before I went with them for a day's adventure. We had a grand time in their motorboat, thundering out of Moffat Cove and skipping from island to island.

We reached Powderhorn Island in the afternoon. As soon as we were ashore, I pulled out the knife. Just as I thought, the McClosky boys were impressed with the superb blade I carried.

With the knife's razor-sharp edge, I hewed out the vague likeness of a boat from a scrap of driftwood. Together, the McCloskys and I rushed to the shore to launch the craft. We pelted it with rocks in a futile attempt to sink it. Our interest died as soon as the boat drifted out of range. Tired of our sport, we returned to the motorboat and headed for home.

It wasn't until the McCloskys had let me off at Moffat Cove and sped away that I remembered my father's knife. It wasn't in my pocket. I had left it on the shore at Powderhorn Island! It was too late in the day for me to return to Powderhorn and get the knife. I would have to wait until tomorrow morning.

8

Now that Friday morning had arrived, I was ready to carry out my mission. My plan was a simple one. All I had to do was row out to Powderhorn in our small skiff, retrieve the knife, and be back in a couple of hours. The knife would be on Father's bureau before he returned today from his business trip. I hoped the knife was still where I had left it. I had no desire to face my father if he found his knife was missing.

I dressed in a hurry and thudded down the stairs. Sally, my six-year-old sister, was sitting in an overstuffed armchair, fiddling with the Rubik's Cube puzzle I had almost solved the night before.

"Put it down, Sally!" I growled as I strode toward the kitchen. "You're messing it all up!"

My mother was standing by the breakfast table, draining the last drops from her coffee cup.

"Good morning, Jason. I'm glad you're awake," she said. "I'm going shopping in Portland before picking up your father at the airport. I need you to watch Sally for me."

"Awwwww, Mom!" I groaned. "Not today! Why can't Sally go with you?"

"It's going to take all day," she replied, "and you know how impatient Sally is about shopping. She would be miserable. So be a dear and keep her happy here at home."

"But, Mom . . . !" I started to protest.

"Jason," she said firmly, "do as I tell you. We'll be back by three o'clock." Then glancing at her wristwatch, she said, "It's getting late. I've got to rush. You behave yourself, Sally," she called out. "Do what Jason tells you to do."

My mother smiled at me as she picked up her purse and left. I walked to the window and watched gloomily as she backed the car out of the driveway. My mission to recover the knife had just been scuttled. I was chained at home to baby-sit my sister!

What could I do now? I wondered. I knew my father's knife lay in plain view on Powderhorn's rocky shore. Anyone might find it and take it. Somehow I had to get to the island, and fast! Only now, I had to devise a plan that included Sally.

"What do you want to do today?" Sally chirped as she bounced into the kitchen.

"Well," I sighed, "I *was* going to row to Powderhorn Island, but now I'm stuck here at home with you."

"Then take me with you," she urged.

"I can't do that. Mom wouldn't like it."

"I won't tell her," she insisted.

"Do you promise?" I asked sternly.

"I promise! Cross my heart."

I studied my sister carefully. Could I really trust her? I wondered. I doubted that I could, but I had to take a chance.

"Okay," I finally agreed, "Get a tin cup. We can pick blueberries while we're there."

Sally smiled her approval and grabbed a cup. Then we walked out of the house together, into the hazy summer morning. A light breeze blew in from the south, bringing with it the smell of the sea and the muffled roar of surf against distant shores. The air was cool and damp, and a bit of morning fog lingered in the cove. But I didn't worry about the fog. I convinced myself that the sun would burn it off in no time.

The hill that sloped down from our house led to a long wooden

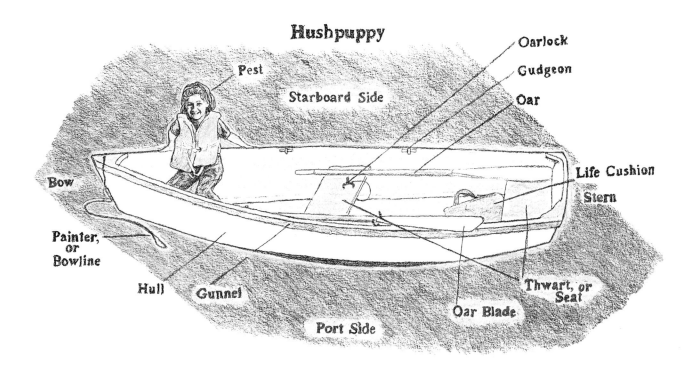

Hushpuppy

Oarlock
Gudgeon
Oar
Pest
Starboard Side
Bow
Life Cushion
Stern
Painter, or Bowline
Hull
Gunnel
Oar Blade
Thwart, or Seat
Port Side

wharf, which was connected by a narrow runway to a float. The float, hinged to rise and fall with the tide, provided a secure place for small boats to be tied.

Sally ran ahead of me, happy to be outside. I stopped off at our boathouse — a damp, dark barn that stood on pilings above the water.

I stepped inside and picked up my sea pouch, an item I always took when I went rowing. The pouch contained necessary survival supplies — a coil of thin strong rope, a lighter, a small box of cookies, a bottle of drinking water, and a compass I had received on my twelfth birthday. Then I jogged to the float where Sally sat perched in the bow of the *Hushpuppy*, our sleek, shallow skiff.

"Buckle your life jacket, Sally," I commanded as I tossed my sea pouch into the boat. Then I threw in a floatable cushion for myself.

I unlashed the skiff from the float, climbed aboard, and carefully lowered myself onto the center seat. I dropped the oarlocks into their gudgeons and shoved off from the float. Then I eased the oars into the oarlocks and started rowing.

The *Hushpuppy* was a lightweight craft that skimmed the surface of the water gracefully, gliding along smoothly and quickly. But with its low sides, I had to be careful. Sharp turns and rogue waves could capsize the small boat.

Ordinarily I liked being out on the water by myself. I enjoyed the sense of control that came with the freedom of choosing where

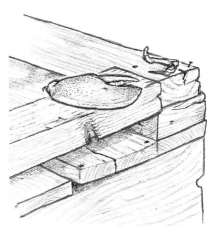

I wanted to go. But not today. I was too preoccupied with retrieving my father's knife. Had I not been so concerned, I might have noticed that the fog over the water was not growing thinner. If anything, the gray mist was getting thicker.

"Jason," Sally whispered, interrupting my thoughts, "go faster! We're about to pass Mr. Grisby's wharf!"

I quickly turned my head and looked toward the wharf. It was a run-down affair that yawned out over the water, supported only by sagging pilings in various stages of decay. It was split and cracked, and covered with leftover bits of decayed lobster shells. It stunk to high heaven!

Everyone tried to avoid going close to Grisby's wharf. They tried to avoid him, too. Grisby was a very unfriendly person, and he certainly didn't like kids. He was well known for shaking his fist in the air and yelling at children.

"Get out of here!" he would shout. "And stay away from my lobster traps, you good-for-nothin' kids!"

The McClosky boys said they weren't afraid of old man Grisby, but I knew better. I saw how they hurried away whenever he came into sight. I didn't mind admitting that I was afraid of the man, and so was Sally.

"Jason, go faster!" Sally pleaded.

Mr. Grisby's big lobster boat was nowhere in sight, which meant he wasn't home. But I started to row faster all the same. With steady, even strokes, the *Hushpuppy* glided away and Grisby's wharf faded into the distance.

I rowed across the calm waters of Ebenecook Bay, aiming for the gap between Spectacle and Boston islands. As the gap passed behind and we entered the Sheepscot River, the crash of surf against the islands grew louder. Far to the south, I could see a blanket of thick fog was lying over the mouth of the river.

The south wind, no longer turned aside by trees and land, hurtled up the Sheepscot. The waves of the open river were choppy, causing our small skiff to pitch and roll. I yelled to Sally to hang on tightly.

Fortunately, Powderhorn Island was not far out into the Sheepscot River. I soon heard Sally squeal, "Jason, there's Powderhorn!" I glanced over my shoulder. The small, treeless island had indeed come into view, sitting like a giant teardrop before us.

I altered our course slightly to head directly for the northern tip of Powderhorn. The oars slashed into the water as I rowed even harder to overcome the Sheepscot's strong current. Before long I

finished our final sprint across the river, rounded the island's tip, and pulled into Powderhorn's tiny cove.

I looked at my wristwatch and found we had made good time. Now all we had to do was pick some blueberries, and, of course, I had to get my father's knife.

"Jason," Sally said, with uneasiness edging into her voice, "isn't that Mr. Grisby's lobster boat?"

I turned quickly and recognized the rust-stained stern and peeling blood-red paint of Grisby's boat! Its stark, chiseled nameplate read *Avenger*. The boat lay in still water, nosed gently onto the beach at the far end of Powderhorn. Its frame seemed to be held together by slime and barnacles. It was a miracle that the pitted hull could float at all.

"Jason!" Sally persisted. "Is that Mr. Grisby's boat, or not?"

"Well, uh, no," I finally stammered, "no, that's not his boat."

"Well, whose boat is it?" she wanted to know.

"I don't know," I replied quickly, trying to avoid frightening her, "but it's not Grisby's."

An overwhelming urge to turn and row away flashed through my mind. But I couldn't leave — not yet. So I rowed the *Hushpuppy* ashore at the opposite end of the beach.

But where was Mr. Grisby? And what would the old lobsterman be doing on an uninhabited island? Whatever it was, I wanted no part of it! Then, calming down a bit, I tried to reassure myself. Although Powderhorn was a small island, there was a good chance that Grisby wouldn't see us. Besides, it should take only a few minutes for me to achieve what I had come to do. Or so I hoped.

I stepped ashore and dragged our skiff onto the beach. Sally hopped out of the *Hushpuppy*, full of energy and exuberance, and carrying her tin cup. I took hold of her hand and led her to a patch of blueberry bushes I had noticed the day before.

"Everyone says the best blueberries grow near the shore," I lied to her. And for a few minutes, I feigned interest in the berries, tasting several of them and commenting on how delicious they were.

"Sally, you pick these berries," I said. "I'll walk over the hill and see if there are more ripe ones on the other side. You stay here. I'll be right back."

"Okay," she answered, already engrossed in eating as many berries as she was putting in the cup.

I got my sea pouch from the skiff and hurried over the hill. Then I made my way through the waist-high brambles until I reached the spot where the McClosky boys and I had been the previous day. And there it was: my father's knife! It lay on the beach, only a few feet away from me. But just as I was about to dart out and get it, I heard a man's rough, gravelly voice. I knew it was Grisby!

"Summer tourists!" I heard him complain loudly. "Fools — all of 'em! Gettin' on their boats and leavin' their brains on land! You'd think they were AIMIN' their motorboats at my buoys, tryin' to slice through my lines on purpose!"

I crouched down and tried to hide in the bushes. I watched the old man come from behind some rocks and amble into clear view along the shore. He was carrying three lobster buoys marked with his individual black color code. Suddenly he stopped and dropped the buoys at his feet. Then he stooped over and tried to tug loose another buoy the high tide had wedged among the rocks.

Now I understood why Grisby was on Powderhorn. He was there to retrieve something, too! He was collecting his wayward buoys that had drifted to the island after their lines had been cut.

"Dratted thing!" Grisby spat, giving the unyielding buoy a fierce yank. Disgusted, he picked up his other buoys and began walking in my direction. The closer he came to me, the more my panic grew. I was sure he would see Father's knife any second. There no longer was any question of my hiding; I had to get the knife before the old man spied it!

When Grisby turned his back to shake his fist at a passing motorboat, I dashed to the rocky shore, scooped up the knife, and scurried back toward the bushes. Grisby never would have known I was there if my pouch hadn't snagged on an old juniper branch. As I frantically ripped the pouch free, I heard the telltale snap of dry wood breaking!

"Who's there?" Grisby growled, turning toward me. "Hey, kid! What are you doing out here?"

Pretending I hadn't heard him, I started running.

Seconds later Grisby called out: "Wait, kid! Come back here!"

But I didn't wait. I didn't even slow down. I headed straight for the beach.

"Sally!" I yelled before I had cleared the brush. "Run to the boat!"

My sister turned and looked at me, but she didn't run. She just stood there with blueberry juice smeared all over her mouth, watching my fast approach.

Without breaking stride, I grabbed Sally's hand and pulled her after me as we rushed pell mell to the *Hushpuppy*. I helped her scramble into the boat. Then I thrust Father's knife into my sea pouch and slung it aboard. I quickly shoved off from the beach, jumped into the skiff, and sat down. The oarlocks were in, the oars were out, and we were on our way, even before Sally had time to sniffle over my rough treatment of her.

I literally dug the oars into the water, making huge trenches in the sea. We rocketed crazily out of Powderhorn's cove. We were no more than fifty yards away when I saw Mr. Grisby lumber onto the beach. He caught sight of us and started toward the water's

16

edge, waving his arms in the air.

"Come back, children!" he called after us. "Come back!"

I wasn't about to do that! I kept rowing as fast as I could.

"What does that man want with us?" Sally asked.

"I don't know," I answered truthfully, "but you put on your life jacket and buckle it!"

"Jason," Sally said in a quavering voice, "isn't that Mr. Grisby?"

"Yes," I answered, nodding my head grimly.

"Then you lied to me! That *was* his lobster boat" she exclaimed in alarm. "And, Jason, look! Mr. Grisby's running to his boat! He's going to get us!"

"Don't worry, he won't catch us," I replied, trying to sound convincing.

We watched as the old man made his way along the beach, untied the bow line of his lobster boat and climbed aboard. Almost immediately we heard him try to start his ancient engine. Mercifully, the motor kept wheezing, coughing, and stalling, giving us a few more precious minutes to escape.

We finally rounded the tip of Powderhorn Island, leaving the cove behind. Now, at least, we were out of Grisby's sight. But, soon we heard the *Avenger's* engine sputter to life and make a loud rumble as Grisby revved the motor several times.

"Jason!" Sally screamed. "He *is* coming after us!"

We watched as the lobster boat came into view from behind Powderhorn. It was indeed heading straight for us and picking up speed. Grisby *was* coming after us! But, why? Why would he be chasing us? I rowed even harder.

Sally was frightened to the point of tears. Though I wouldn't want to admit it, so was I. I was so upset I hadn't realized that the fog had crept so far upriver. Carried upstream by the south wind, the wall of gray mist had rolled in and almost obscured the nearby islands. And it was rapidly settling over us.

Ordinarily fog is a danger to be avoided at any cost, but on that day, I welcomed it. I reasoned that it might be our salvation. If I could beat Grisby into the thick fog, I might have a chance to lose him there.

The light, sleek *Hushpuppy* was no slow boat, and with my desperate need to escape, I soon widened the distance between us and the *Avenger's* faltering engine. But then, Grisby threw his throttle wide open, and the lobster boat came chugging after us. The gap between us began to narrow. Even the strongest rower could not compete for long with a tireless piece of machinery. But I tried even

harder, and the *Hushpuppy* finally shot like an arrow into the fog.

As soon as the fog had closed over our stern, I angled our skiff into a sharp right-angle turn. Water lapped dangerously over the side as the shallow craft dug into the waves.

"Hang on tight, Sally!" I shouted.

The fog diffused the noise of Grisby's motor, bouncing its rumble off every little water particle, making sounds like a thousand *Avengers* were bearing down on us. I bit my lip in unashamed fright.

In desperation, I changed course again and swerved to the left. The fog now enclosed us in a tight circle of limited visibility. I assumed that Mr. Grisby's boat was surrounded by fog, too. But after a few tortured minutes of zigs and zags, I outmaneuvered the old lobsterman, and he finally lost our trail. From somewhere in the distance, we heard one last call of "Children, where are you?" before the drone of Grisby's engine faded away, and he was gone.

Sally, terrified from the ordeal, was sobbing softly.

I tried to comfort her. "It's all right now, Sally," I said. "Mr. Grisby's gone."

Then, exhausted, I pulled in the oars and tried to catch my breath for a few minutes. I had some feeling of satisfaction because I had outwitted Grisby and escaped from him.

I looked at my watch. It was 12:00 noon. I had three hours — plenty of time to get home before my parents returned. All I had to do now was head east until I reached Boston Island, then follow its shoreline through the gap and row across Ebenecook Bay to Moffat Cove. The fact that I was utterly lost, with nearly zero visibility, didn't bother me much. I knew I could rely on my compass.

I pulled my sea pouch from under the seat, reached inside it, and began searching for the compass. Something was wrong! My compass wasn't there!

My heart pounded frantically as I searched every inch of the pouch, pulling out the box of cookies, the coil of rope, the lighter, and the bottle of water. Only my father's knife remained inside. But where was the compass? I wondered. I had to have it! I couldn't navigate in the fog without it! How would we get home?

"Jason, why aren't we moving anymore?" Sally asked.

"Be quiet, Sally," I replied. "I need time to think."

I did need time to think. My headlong rush into the fog had left me completely disoriented. I didn't know north from south. Without being able to see any landmarks, and with no compass to guide me, I had to figure out another way to get us back to Moffat Cove.

"Jason, is Mr. Grisby going to get us now?"

"SALLY, BE QUIET!" I snapped.

Sally instantly cowered into the folds of her life jacket and said, "Don't be mad at me, Jason. I'm so scared."

"I'm not mad at you, Sally," I said, trying to calm down. "But, *please* be quiet and let me think!"

As I replaced the items in my pouch, I carefully considered my options. Which of my five senses could I use to guide me home? Sight was out. Smell might help, but I could detect no distinctive odors. And the fog would amplify and distort sound, so I ruled out hearing, too. Taste? I certainly couldn't taste my way home. Touch? What could I touch to tell me the way home? Not the

19

water, nor the boat. But, wait a minute, I could *feel* the wind! Maybe . . . just maybe . . . I could use the wind that had been blowing from the south all day. If I kept that south wind on the right, starboard side of the boat, I could still reach Boston Island and find my way home!

It would work! I thought proudly. Although the wind had diminished and was at times barely perceptible, I could still use it. So I began rowing briskly, guiding the skiff through the fog while the breeze continued to lightly caress the starboard side.

"Jason, may I ask a question now?" Sally said quietly.

"Sure," I replied. "What do you want to know?"

"Where is Mr. Grisby now?"

"Mr. Grisby went home," I assured her.

"When are we going to get home?"

"In about an hour," I answered confidently.

"But I'm hungry! I want to be home NOW!" she whined.

"Look in my sea pouch, Sally. You'll find some cookies in there."

Sally picked up the pouch and pulled out the box of cookies. "These aren't chocolate chip," she said with a pout, "but I guess I'll eat some anyway."

After gobbling down a few cookies, Sally launched into an irritating, off-key rendition of *Twinkle, Twinkle, Little Star.* The sound of my oars made a steady beat as I tried to ignore her. My concentration had to remain riveted to the only lifeline I had — the wind.

My body performed the mechanical chore of rowing — pull, lift, push back, pull, lift, push back. The motion finally had an almost hypnotic effect upon me. I barely noticed when Sally began singing *Little Bunny Foo Foo,* which was definitely not my favorite song.

Suddenly a large drop of seawater smacked my chin. It startled me. I shook my head, feeling like I had been awakened from a long nap. I bent over and wiped my face on my sleeve, then looked at my watch. My jaw went slack as I stared in horror at the dial. It read 1:25!

Something was wrong — terribly wrong! This morning it had taken me less than an hour to row from Moffat Cove to Powderhorn. But, on the way back, I had been rowing for more than an hour and still not reached Boston Island! Even if we had gone a little bit off course, I told myself, surely I would have seen one of the islands that lay in the vicinity.

The full impact of our predicament hit me, then, like an iron fist of despair and desperation. We were lost in dense fog without a com-

pass, and I only had a little over an hour to get home before my parents returned! Not knowing what else to do, I started rowing again, making sure the wind was blowing on the starboard side of our boat. Sally, her strength fortified by the rest of the cookies, switched to *Row, Row, Row Your Boat.* How appropriate, I thought wryly.

The oars, the slapping of waves against the side of the skiff, Sally's off-key voice, and the dull roar of surf blended together. The sounds seemed to reverberate and echo from all sides of the gray nothingness, coming from everywhere, yet nowhere.

As I rowed on, my uneasiness increased. Nothing seemed right. I became even more disturbed when the sound of surf grew louder. I couldn't remember ever having heard surf crash like that against Boston Island. But if we weren't near Boston Island, where were we?

As I pondered the situation, I noticed something in the water was creeping up behind our skiff. A seal, perhaps? I rowed on, watching as the object steadily neared our stern. Then I recognized it: it was a lobster buoy! But this was impossible! I thought. Lobster buoys were tied to heavily weighted traps that rested on the bottom of the sea. A lobster buoy could not possibly catch up to us while we were rowing away from it!

Even so, the buoy did keep following us, and as it started to move past our skiff, I yelled: "Sally! Grab that lobster buoy!"

Sally, startled out of her song, did exactly what I told her to do. I pulled in the oars and tied the buoy to our bow line. Now, like the buoy, the *Hushpuppy* was anchored to the underwater trap and held in place. I noticed the black paint on the buoy. Wouldn't you know! It belonged to Grisby! What evil coincidence was this? I wondered.

If the gray blanket of fog had lifted right at that moment, I would have discovered immediately that the wind had shifted. No longer was it blowing from the south; it was coming from the east. That change of direction had fooled me into heading back up the Sheepscot River. I had been rowing in the wrong direction! And I had been steadily rowing into a current that was so powerful, it had forced me downstream while I was trying to row upstream. The current, pulling us against the taut line of the lobster trap, was proof of that.

And I did realize all of this eventually, as I sat there with our skiff tied to Grisby's lobster buoy, floating somewhere in the middle of the Sheepscot River. What was really scary was that the strong current of the river held us in its grasp. If I untied the *Hushpuppy* from the buoy, we would be carried out to sea on a one-way trip. What could I do? I wondered. If ever I needed a good plan, it was now!

I probably could row faster than the current of the Sheepscot for a brief sprint, but not for long. Still, I couldn't stay tied to the lobster buoy and wait for the fog to lift; that could take all night and into tomorrow. Not only would Father find his knife was missing; he would find his children were missing, as well.

I decided to brave the current and row across it. Yes, we would be carried sideways downriver, but at some point, we would eventually reach the eastern edge of the Sheepscot, near Southport Island. I tried to convince myself that anything was better than staying where we were.

So I untied the line from the buoy and started rowing again, this time directly into the east wind. Fifteen minutes seemed like fifteen hours to my aching arms. But when I heard surf crashing somewhere nearby, my hopes began to rise. I knew we were close to a shore, but which shore?

I heaved the skiff toward the sound, glancing frequently over my shoulder, waiting for the image of land to appear out of the fog. I watched wave after wave come up under us and slowly make its peaceful way out of my field of vision. Finally, a wave swept beneath the *Hushpuppy*, and I turned and watched it boom and fragment upon the harsh, jagged rocks that suddenly loomed in front of our frail skiff.

I realized those rocks provided no safe place for us to land. They held only a promise to crush our small boat. I pulled heavily on my right oar so our skiff would turn around, then started rowing like mad away from the island. Finally, we were far enough from land to escape the pull of the surf that threatened to throw us against the dark shore.

I still didn't know where we were, except we weren't at Boston Island. Boston had no crashing surf. And in the hazy fog, I had seen trees, but no houses, so I knew we weren't at Southport Island either. Southport definitely had houses near its shore. I felt tired and utterly defeated, but I continued to row on.

After a while, I heard Sally say in a scolding voice: "Jason, you didn't wave back!"

"Wave back at what?" I asked with disinterest.

"At the Wavy Oak," she answered, pointing toward the east.

My eyes widened, and I turned to look directly at her.

"Sally, did you *really* see the Wavy Oak?"

"Yeah!" she exclaimed. "He was standing right over there, and he waved back at me."

The Wavy Oak was an old, twisted, dead oak tree that stood on Far Green Island. Mom and Sally said it looked like a ghost that liked to wave to passers-by. Sally always made a point of waving to the tree.

"Sally, are you *sure* it was the Wavy Oak?"

"Yes, I'm sure. I know what Wavy Oak looks like."

If Sally was right, I knew where we were — just a short distance off Far Green Island! There was dangerous surf there. But if I could maneuver the *Hushpuppy* in between the narrow passage that lay between Far Green and nearby Main Green Island, our skiff could make it into the calmer waters of Ebenecook Bay. From there, we could easily cross to Moffat Cove.

With renewed determination, I rowed a little south of what I hoped was the location of Far Green Island, aiming our skiff toward the channel between the islands. Slowly, so slowly, Far Green Island came into view. Then the silhouette of Main Green gradually materialized out of the mist.

Luck was with us! I had lined up our skiff perfectly. We soon entered the channel, and the *Hushpuppy* made its painstaking way between the two islands. As we passed through the waterway, the roaring surf and jagged rocks of Far Green and Main Green islands framed our skiff.

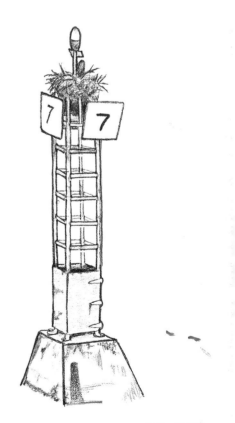

Thankfully, it was much easier rowing here than in the strong current of the Sheepscot River. And having visual reference points, I no longer had to rely solely on the shifting wind for direction. I kept our course through the narrow channel and finally brought us into the safe waters of Ebenecook Bay.

Then I looked at my watch again and stopped rowing in mid-stroke. "Two-thirty!" I gasped. "No wonder I'm so exhausted!" I had been rowing for two and a half hours! Nevertheless, I had to keep moving. My parents would be home in thirty minutes. If we weren't there, I would be in big trouble!

I had escaped from Mr. Grisby and maneuvered our skiff through the fog without a compass. But I knew Mom and Dad would be in no mood to congratulate me for my accomplishments.

"You should have stayed home where you belonged...," they would say.

I grimaced at the thought and started rowing into the east wind as vigorously as my tired arms would allow. After about ten minutes of singing *There's a Hole in the Bottom of the Sea*, Sally

25

stopped her miserable warbling and called out, "There's the Ink Bottle!" the name given to a small automatic lighthouse on the western approach to Moffat Cove.

We were close to home! But I couldn't stop to rest now. I continued rowing feverishly, frequently glancing at my watch. My body was crying out with pain when our wharf came into view.

Finally, triumphant, I pulled up to the float. I was exhausted, but happily so. Though my body was drenched in sweat, I had prevailed against the elements. Without compass, with only my wits, I had found my way home from Powderhorn in thick fog.

But it was ten minutes until three o'clock.

I only had ten minutes to return my Father's knife!

I grabbed my sea pouch and climbed out of the *Hushpuppy*. Then I lashed the boat to her proper place along the float, using the fastest half-hitch knot I had ever tied.

"Come on, Sally, hurry!" I ordered, grabbing hold of her hand and pulling her onto the float. Then we dashed up the runway and across the wharf. As we raced up the hill to the farmhouse, I looked at my watch.

Seven minutes until three!

Sally was right behind me as I wrenched open the back door. I sped across the kitchen and into the living room. I exhaled in sharp relief; Mom and Dad had not yet returned home.

Taking the steps two at a time, I ran upstairs to my parents' bedroom. I took Father's knife from the sea pouch and carefully placed it on his bureau.

After tossing the pouch behind my bedroom door, I rushed back downstairs to the living room. Sweat was dripping from my face. I wiped it away with my sleeve, grabbed a book, and assumed a relaxed position on the couch.

My sister entered the room and sat down directly across from me in the same overstuffed chair she had vacated that morning. I sat up straight, then leaned forward and looked intently at her.

"Now, remember, Sally," I reminded her, "you promised not to tell Mom and Dad that we rowed out to Powderhorn today."

"Oh . . . did I promise that?" she asked, pretending to forget.

"You know you did," I replied sharply.

"What will you give me not to tell?" she whined as she picked up my Rubik's Cube and held it in her hand.

So that's how it was going to be, I thought to myself.

"Okay, Sally, you may play with my Rubik's Cube," I replied with a sigh.

"Thanks," she said, giving me a smug smile and settling back contentedly in the chair.

We heard the back door open and Mom's clear "Hello!" ring through the house. "We're back," she said, entering the room with her arms full of packages. "The fog is awful! I'm glad your father's flight wasn't delayed, but we had to be extra careful driving back. I was relieved to know that the two of you were safe here at home. How did everything go today?"

I forced myself to look directly at my mother's face, then answered, "Oh...ah...fine, Mom."

Sally kept an innocent, angelic look on her face and said sweetly, "Jason's been real nice to me all day, haven't you, Jason? He's even letting me play with his Rubik's Cube."

"I'm glad to hear that," Mom replied with a smile. Then she hurried upstairs to put away her purchases.

Dad carried his suitcase into the room and said, "Hi, guys," before he followed Mom upstairs to unpack.

Sally just sat there smiling at me, giving me that we-know-something-Mom-and-Dad-don't-know kind of look.

I glared at my sister with complete disgust. The whole terrible day had taken its toll on me. I felt numb all over.

The doorbell rang, and I got up automatically and went to answer it. When I pulled open the door and looked outside, I gasped! Standing on the porch was the rugged form of none other than Mr. Grisby! A slight smile crept across his weathered face.

"Well, there you are, lad," he said. "Glad to see you made it home safely. I was sure you'd get lost in that fog without this."

In his outstretched hand lay my compass.

"You dropped it on Powderhorn today," he said.

"It...it must have fallen out of my sea pouch," I stammered nervously, for I was dumbfounded by his unexpected friendliness.

"I called to you," the old man said. "Guess you didn't hear me."

"Thank you, Mr. Grisby," I replied as I reached out and took my compass from him. "It's nice of you to bring it to me."

"No trouble," he chuckled. "You must be a good sailor to make it through that fog without a compass."

"I try to be," I replied.

"Well, be seein' ya," he said, and he turned and stepped off the porch, his hands thrust deep into his pockets. I watched the old lobsterman walk away. I couldn't believe he had been so kind to me.

"You must be a good sailor," he had said.

Well, I guess I was a pretty good sailor, and I was proud of that. But in the last two days, I had been good at a number of other things I wasn't so proud of. I had been a good thief. I had been a

good liar. I had involved my sister in a scheme that had put us both in danger. I had even persuaded Sally to lie to our parents. And by getting her to tell a lie, I had given my six-year-old sister the power to blackmail me.

This has gone too far, I told myself. It's got to stop, and I'm going to stop it right now! I shut the back door, walked over to Sally, and took the Rubik's Cube out of her hands. Then I went upstairs to my parents' room.

"Mom, Dad," I said resolutely, "I need to tell you what happened today."

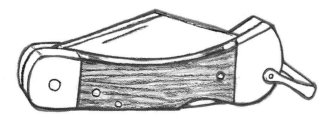

BOOKS FOR STUDENTS

– WINNERS OF THE NATIONAL WRITTEN &

A Chandrasekhar
age 9

Anika Thomas
age 13

Cara Reichel
age 15

Jonathan Kahn
age 9

Adam Moore
age 9

Leslie A MacKeen
age 9

Elizabeth Haidle
age 13

Amy Hagstrom
age 9

Isaac Whitlatch
age 11

Dav Pilkey
age 19

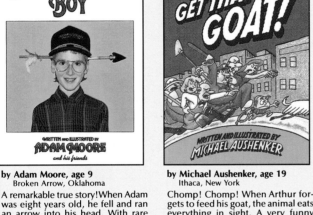

by Aruna Chandrasekhar, age 9
Houston, Texas

A touching and timely story! When the lives of many otters are threatened by a huge oil spill, a group of concerned people come to their rescue. Wonderful illustrations.
Printed Full Color
ISBN 0-933849-33-8

by Anika D. Thomas, age 13
Pittsburgh, Pennsylvania

A compelling autobiography! A young girl's heartrending account of growing up in a tough, inner-city neighborhood. The illustrations match the mood of this gripping story.
Printed Two Colors
ISBN 0-933849-34-6

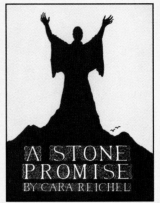

by Cara Reichel, age 15
Rome, Georgia

Elegant and eloquent! A young stonecutter vows to create a great statue for his impoverished village. But his fame almost stops him from fulfilling that promise.
Printed Two Colors
ISBN 0-933849-35-4

by Jonathan Kahn, age 9
Richmond Heights, Ohio

A fascinating nature story! Whi Patulous, a prairie rattlesnak searches for food, he must try avoid the claws and fangs of his ow enemies.
Printed Full Color
ISBN 0-933849-36-2

by Adam Moore, age 9
Broken Arrow, Oklahoma

A remarkable true story! When Adam was eight years old, he fell and ran an arrow into his head. With rare insight and humor, he tells of his ordeal and his amazing recovery.
Printed Two Colors
ISBN 0-933849-24-9

by Michael Aushenker, age 19
Ithaca, New York

Chomp! Chomp! When Arthur forgets to feed his goat, the animal eats everything in sight. A very funny story — good to the last bite. The illustrations are terrific.
Printed Full Color
ISBN 0-933849-28-1

by Leslie Ann MacKeen, age 9
Winston-Salem, North Carolina

Loaded with fun and puns! When Jeremiah T. Fitz's car stops running, several animals offer suggestions for fixing it. The results are hilarious. The illustrations are charming.
Printed Full Color
ISBN 0-933849-19-2

by Elizabeth Haidle, age 13
Beaverton, Oregon

A very touching story! The grum iest Elfkin learns to cherish th friendship of others after he help an injured snail and befriends orphaned boy. Absolutely beautifu
Printed Full Color
ISBN 0-933849-20-6

by Amy Hagstrom, age 9
Portola, California

An exciting western! When a boy and an old Indian try to save a herd of wild ponies, they discover a lost canyon and see the mystical vision of the Great White Stallion.
Printed Full Color
ISBN 0-933849-15-X

by Isaac Whitlatch, age 11
Casper, Wyoming

The true confessions of a devout vegetable hater! Isaac tells ways to avoid and dispose of the "slimy green things." His colorful illustrations provide a salad of laughter and mirth.
Printed Full Color
ISBN 0-933849-16-8

by Dav Pilkey, age 19
Cleveland, Ohio

A thought-provoking parable! Two kings halt an arms race and learn to live in peace. This outstanding book launched Dav's career. He now has seven more books published.
Printed Full Color
ISBN 0-933849-22-2

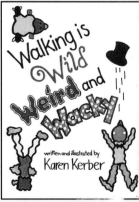

by Karen Kerber, age 12
St. Louis, Missouri

A delightfully playful book! The te is loaded with clever alliterations a gentle humor. Karen's brightly c ored illustrations are composed wiggly and waggly strokes of geniu
Printed Full Color
ISBN 0-933849-29-X

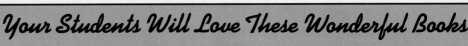

Your Students Will Love These Wonderful Books

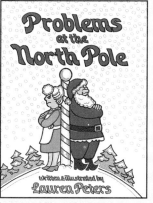

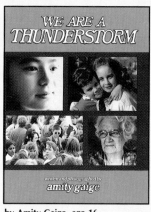
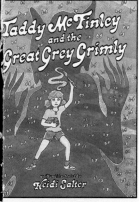
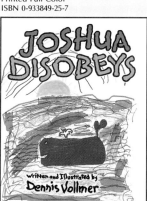

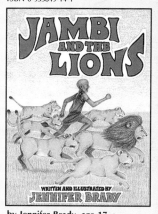

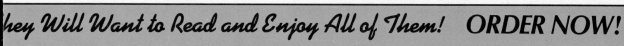

THE WINNERS OF THE 1992 NATIONAL
WRITTEN & ILLUSTRATED BY... AWARDS FOR STUDENTS

FIRST PLACE	**FIRST PLACE**	**FIRST PLACE**	**GOLD AWARD**	**GOLD AWARD**
6–9 Age Category	10–13 Age Category	14–19 Age Category	Publisher's Selection	Publisher's Selection
Benjamin Kendall	**Steven Shepard**	**Travis Williams**	**Dubravka Kolanovic'**	**Amy Jones**
age 7	age 13	age 16	age 18	age 17
State College, Pennsylvania	Great Falls, Virginia	Sardis, B.C., Canada	Savannah, Georgia	Shirley, Arkansas

 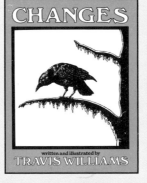  

ALIEN INVASIONS
When Ben puts on a new super-hero costume, he starts seeing Aliens who are from outer space. His attempts to stop the pesky invaders provide loads of laughs. The colorful illustrations add to the fun!

29 Pages, Full Color
ISBN 0-933849-42-7

FOGBOUND
A gripping thriller! When a boy rows his boat to an island to retrieve a stolen knife, he must face threatening fog, treacherous currents, and a sinister lobsterman. Outstanding illustrations!

29 Pages, Two-Color
ISBN 0-933849-43-5

CHANGES
A chilling mystery! When a teen-age boy discovers his classmates are missing, he becomes entrapped in a web of conflicting stories, false alibis, and frightening changes. Dramatic ink drawings!

29 Pages, Two-Color
ISBN 0-933849-44-3

A SPECIAL DAY
Ivan enjoys a wonderful day in the country with his grandparents, a dog, a cat, and a delightful bear that is *always* hungry. Cleverly written, brilliantly illustrated! Little kids will love this book!

29 Pages, Full Color
ISBN 0-933849-45-1

ABRACADABRA
A whirlwind adventure! An enchanted unicorn helps a young girl rescue her eccentric aunt from the evil Sultan of Zabar. A charming story, with lovely illustrations that add a magical glow!

29 Pages, Full Color
ISBN 0-933849-46-X

BOOKS FOR STUDENTS BY STUDENTS!®

Written & Illustrated by...
by David Melton

This highly acclaimed teacher's manual offers classroom-proven, step-by-step instructions in all aspects of teaching students how to write, illustrate, assemble, and bind original books. Loaded with information and positive approaches that really work. Contains lesson plans, more than 200 illustrations, and suggested adaptations for use at all grade levels — K through college.

The results are dazzling!
Children's Book Review Service, Inc.

WRITTEN & ILLUSTRATED BY... provides a current of enthusiasm, positive thinking and faith in the creative spirit of children. David Melton has the heart of a teacher.
THE READING TEACHER

...an exceptional book! Just browsing through it stimulates excitement for writing.
Joyce E. Juntune, Executive Director
The National Association for Creativity

A "how to" book that really works.
Judy O'Brien, Teacher

Softcover, 96 Pages
ISBN 0-933849-00-1

LANDMARK EDITIONS, INC.
P.O. BOX 4469 • KANSAS CITY, MISSOURI 64127 • (816) 241-4919